W9-CDO-515

Bajo las olas/Under the Sea

Caballitos de mar/Sea Horses

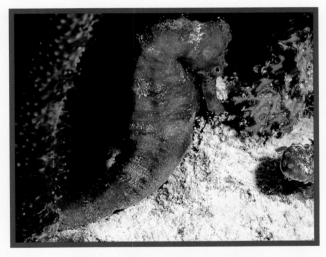

por/by Carol K. Lindeen

Traducción/Translation: Dr. Martín Luis Guzmán Ferrer

Editor Consultor/Consulting Editor: Dra. Gail Saunders-Smith

Consultor/Consultant: Jody Rake, Member
Southwest Marine/Aquatic Educators' Association

Capstone
press
Mankato, Minnesota

Pebble Plus is published by Capstone Press,
151 Good Counsel Drive, P.O. Box 669, Mankato, Minnesota 56002.
www.capstonepress.com

1 2 3 4 5 6 12 11 10 09 08 07

Library of Congress Cataloging-in-Publication Data
Lindeen, Carol K., 1976–
   [Sea horses. Spanish & English]
   Caballitos de mar = Sea horses/por/by Carol K. Lindeen.
   p. cm.—(Pebble plus: Bajo las olas = Under the sea)
   Includes index.
   ISBN-13: 978-0-7368-7647-6 (hardcover)
   ISBN-10: 0-7368-7647-2 (hardcover)
   1. Sea horses—Juvenile literature. I. Title. II. Title: Sea horses. III. Series.
QL638.S9L5618 2007
597'.6798—dc22   2006027851

Summary: Simple text and photographs present sea horses, their body parts, and their behavior—in both
   English and Spanish.

Editorial Credits
Martha E. H. Rustad, editor; Katy Kudela, bilingual editor; Eida del Risco, Spanish copy editor; Juliette Peters,
   set designer; Kate Opseth, book designer; Kelly Garvin, photo researcher; Scott Thoms, photo editor

Photo Credits
Bruce Coleman Inc./Masa Ushioda, 8–9
Corbis RF/Marty Snyderman, 1; Amos Nachoum, 6–7
Herb Segars, cover
Minden Pictures/Birgitte Wilms, 10–11; Fred Bavendam, 18–19; Norbert Wu, 14–15, 20–21
Seapics.com/Bob Cranston, 4–5; Lines Jr./Shedd Aquarium, 12–13; Rudie Kuiter, 16–17

Note to Parents and Teachers

The Bajo las olas/Under the Sea set supports national science standards related to the
diversity and unity of life. This book describes and illustrates sea horses in both English
and Spanish. The images support early readers in understanding the text. The repetition
of words and phrases helps early readers learn new words. This book also introduces
early readers to subject-specific vocabulary words, which are defined in the Glossary
section. Early readers may need assistance to read some words and to use the Table of
Contents, Glossary, Internet Sites, and Index sections of the book.

Table of Contents

Tabla de contenidos

What Are Sea Horses?

Sea horses are fish.

¿Qué son los caballitos de mar?

Los caballitos de mar

son peces.

Sea horses are about
as long as a new pencil.

Los caballitos de mar
son tan largos como
un lápiz nuevo.

Body Parts

The head of a sea horse

looks like the head

of a horse.

Las partes del cuerpo

La cabeza del caballito

de mar se parece a

la cabeza de un caballo.

Bony plates cover sea horses.
The plates help keep
sea horses safe.

Unas placas óseas cubren al
caballito de mar. Las placas sirven
para proteger al caballito de mar.

plate/
placa

11

Sea horses have fins.

They move their fins to swim.

Los caballitos de mar tienen
aletas. Mueven las aletas
para nadar.

fin/
aleta

Sea horses have curly tails.
They hold on to plants
with their tails.

Los caballitos de mar tienen
la cola ondulada. Con la cola
se sujetan de las plantas.

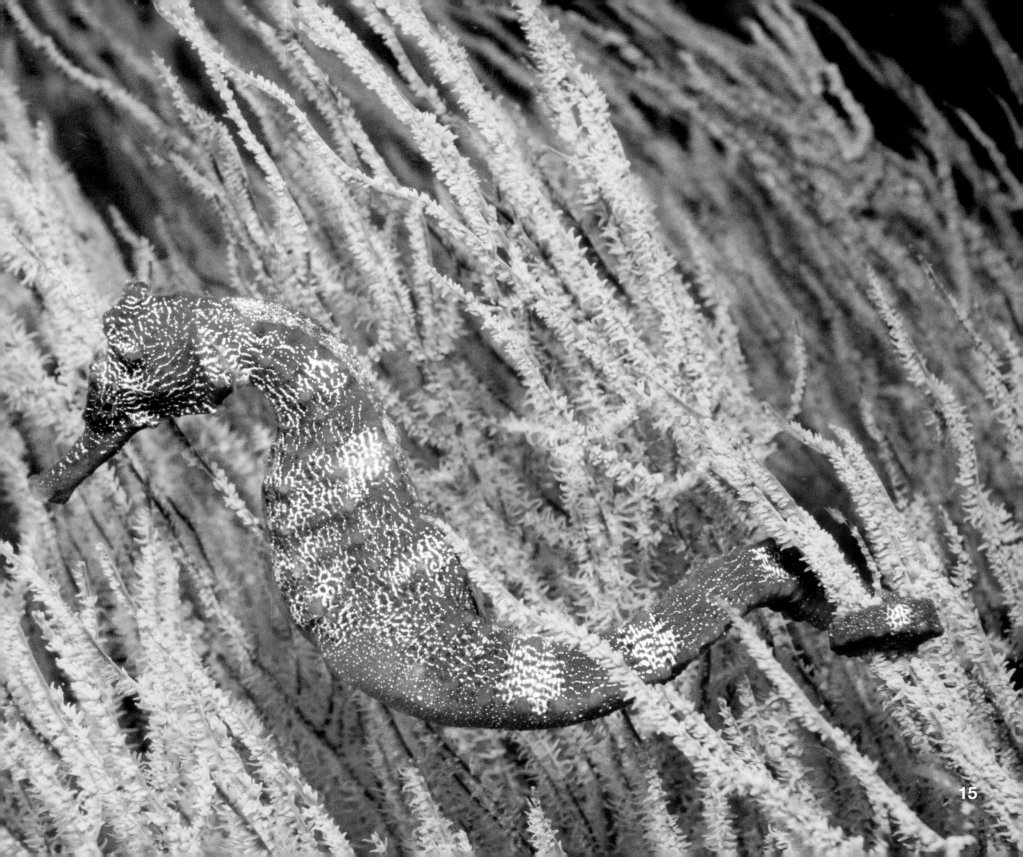

What Sea Horses Do

Sea horses hold on

to each other

with their tails.

Qué hacen los caballitos de mar

Los caballitos de mar se

sujetan unos de otros

con las colas.

Sea horses can change color.

They hide near plants.

Los caballitos de mar
pueden cambiar de color.

Se esconden entre las plantas.

Under the Sea

Sea horses swim

in shallow water

under the sea.

Bajo las olas

Los caballitos de mar

nadan en aguas

poco profundas.

Glossary

bony—hard like a bone

curly—curved or twisted

fin—a body part that fish use to swim and steer in water

fish—a cold-blooded animal that lives in water and has fins and gills

plate—a hard covering on an animal's body that helps keep it safe

shallow—not very deep

Glosario

la aleta—parte del cuerpo que los peces usan para nadar y girar

ondulado—curvo o torcido

óseo—duro como un hueso

el pez—animal de sangre fría que vive en el agua y tiene agallas

la placa—cubierta dura en el cuerpo de un animal que sirve para protegerlo

poco profundo—no muy hondo

Internet Sites

FactHound offers a safe, fun way to find Internet sites related to this book. All of the sites on FactHound have been researched by our staff.

Here's how:

1. Visit *www.facthound.com*

2. Choose your grade level.

3. Type in this book ID **0736876472** for age-appropriate sites. You may also browse subjects by clicking on letters, or by clicking on pictures and words.

4. Click on the **Fetch It** button.

FactHound will fetch the best sites for you!

Index

Sitios de Internet

FactHound proporciona una manera divertida y segura de encontrar sitios de Internet relacionados con este libro. Nuestro personal ha investigado todos los sitios de FactHound. Es posible que los sitios no estén en español.

Se hace así:

1. Visita *www.facthound.com*

2. Elige tu grado escolar.

3. Introduce este código especial **0736876472** para ver sitios apropiados según tu edad, o usa una palabra relacionada con este libro para hacer una búsqueda general.

4. Haz clic en el botón **Fetch It**.

¡FactHound buscará los mejores sitios para ti!

Índice